good morning Franny ♡ good night Franny

by Emily Hearn

Illustrations by Mark Thurman

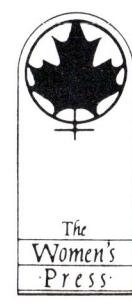

The Women's Press

SPRING! I can hear the street-watering truck. That means there's no more snow. And that means I can go for walks by myself. Now!

Chirp, SPLASH! CAW, CAW, WHIRRRRRRRRRRR

Hurry up, elevator.
3, 2, 1 ... Liftoff!

Mr. Becks teases me as he holds the door open.
"Don't go breaking any speed records," he says.
"Not this time," I agree.
He knows what happened to me last summer.
I'll tell you about that.

I felt like I do today, full of zip,
and so glad to be on my own that I let fly ...

faster ... faster...
past the apartments ...
then the church ...

... the old mansion that's little offices now ...

I sped round the corner by the doughnut shop and WHAM!
I really did it, I knocked over the pigeon-lady's cart.

Parcels of bread and grain that she feeds the pigeons
were everywhere on the sidewalk.
She was furious with me.
What could I do?
A little girl came over
and helped
put it all
back.

"Just don't go fast like that again, not watching where you're going," the pigeon-lady grumbled as she stomped off.

"I won't," I promised, ashamed of myself, "I won't."

"Thanks," I said to the little girl.
I remembered seeing her before, drawing, as she sat on
 a milk crate in front of the variety store.
"Good morning," she said, slowly, formally.
"Good morning," I replied. "What's your name?"
When she didn't answer I pointed to myself. "I'm Franny."
She smiled shyly, then said "Ting."

I patted my lap. "Want a ride, Ting?"
She understood that!
She scooted back for her colouring book, gave a little bounce and squeezed in with me.

You'd think we were royalty the way she sat up on our throne, giggling and waving to Mr. Khan at the restaurant, to Maria at her fruit stand.

We rounded the corner to the park.
Ting hopped down and climbed on a swing.
I gave her a push to get her started.
Soon she was pumping as high as the circling pigeons.

I took her crayon and printed TING and FRANNY
    under a picture of us both that I drew in her scrapbook.
She liked that.
Before lunch I took her back to the store.
"Goodnight Franny," she said slowly, formally.
"Goodnight Ting," I waved to her. "See you again!"

et often.

"Good morning," she'd say, then show me the frisbee or ball she had taken from the store for us to play with in the park.

She liked to surprise me.

...e really proud the windy day we actually got the
...tterfly kite up in the air.
...e'd always draw in her book before going back, and she
would work away trying to print some of the words I
showed her.

I had to go into the hospital near summer's end, for some tests.
I told Ting about it, but I'm not sure that she knew what I meant.
The nurses let me keep a picture book that I liked reading when I was there.

Right after I got home I set out with it to show Ting.
I tried to remember not to speed on the hill and
not to whiz around that corner ...

But there was no milk crate.
There was no Ting.
Just an empty store with a sign saying CLOSED.
I asked Mr. Khan.
"That's the way it is with business," he shrugged,
   "too hard to make it pay these days. Nobody knows
   where the Kims have gone."
I went around to the park. You can bet I was crying.

But Ting had left another surprise for me.
She must have sneaked paint from her dad's store because ...

on the pavement going into the park it said ...
Good Morning Franny.

Look! It's months later and the printing stayed all winter, under all that snow! See? And where I go back out of the park she wrote ...

Good night Franny.

Good morning Ting.
Good night, wherever you are!

EMILY HEARN loves to create for young people. She writes music, poetry, radio and television programs, does a comic strip with Mark and develops wonderful storybooks like *Good Morning Franny, Good Night Franny*.

MARK THURMAN is an artist who helps girls and boys with their drawing. He works with Emily on a popular comic strip about the adventures of the 'Mighty Mites', and enjoys illustrating picture books for young readers.